My dear mouse friends,

Have I ever told you how much I love science fiction? I've always wanted to write incredible adventures set in another dimension, but I've never believed that parallel universes exist . . . until now!

That's because my good friend Professor Paws von Volt, the brilliant, secretive scientist, has just made an incredible discovery. Thanks to some mousetropic calculations, he determined that there are many different dimensions in time and space, where anything could be possible.

The professor's work inspired me to write this science fiction adventure in which my family and I travel through space in search of new worlds. We're a fabumouse crew: the spacemice!

I hope you enjoy this intergalactic adventure!

Geronimo Stilton

**PROFESSOR
PAWS VON VOLT**

THE SPACEMICE

GERONIMO STILTONIX

TRAP STILTONIX

THEA STILTONIX

GRANDFATHER WILLIAM STILTONIX

ROBOTIX

BENJAMIN STILTONIX AND BUGSY WUGSY

Geronimo Stilton

SPACEMICE

YOU'RE MINE, CAPTAIN!

Scholastic Inc.

ISBN 978-0-545-64652-9

Based on an original idea by Elisabetta Dami.

www.geronimostilton.com

Published by Scholastic Inc., 557 Broadway, New York, NY 10012. SCHOLASTIC and associated logos are trademarks and/or registered trademarks of Scholastic Inc.

Stilton is the name of a famous English cheese. It is a registered trademark of the Stilton Cheese Makers' Association. For more information, go to www.stiltoncheese.com.

Text by Geronimo Stilton
Original title *Un'aliena per il Capitano Stiltonix*
Cover by Flavio Ferron
Interior illustrations by Giuseppe Facciotto (design)
and Daniele Verzini (color)
Graphics by Chiara Cebraro

Special thanks to Shannon Penney
Translated by Julia Heim
Interior design by Joseph Semien

12 11 10 9 8 7 6 5 4 3 2 1   14 15 16 17 18 19/0

Printed in the U.S.A.   40
First printing, August 2014

In the darkness of the farthest galaxy in time and space is a spaceship inhabited exclusively by mice.

This fabumouse vessel is called the **MouseStar 1**, and I am its captain!

I am Geronimo Stiltonix, a somewhat accident-prone mouse who (to tell you the truth) would rather be writing novels than steering a spaceship.

But for now, my adventurous family and I are busy traveling around the universe on exciting intergalactic missions.

THIS IS THE LATEST ADVENTURE OF THE SPACEMICE!

A Strange, Strange Noise . . .

It all started one stellar afternoon on my spaceship, the *MouseStar 1*. I was in my cabin working on my *book* . . . when suddenly, I heard a strange, strange noise: *Grumble!*

"Holey craters! What was that?" I squeaked. "A Martian *invader*? An alien slug slipping in through a porthole? A carnivorous bloboid that escaped from Pluto?"

My whiskers trembled in fright!

I looked under the bed . . . NOTHING!

I checked behind the curtains . . . NOTHING!

I looked all around my desk . . . NOTHING there, either! Just the notes for the book that I was writing: *The Amazing Adventures of the Spacemice.*

Oh, pardon me — I haven't introduced myself! My name is Stiltonix, **Geronimo Stiltonix**. I am the captain of the *MouseStar 1*, the most mouserific *spaceship* in the universe. It's a fabumouse job, but my SECRET dream is to be an author!

As I was saying, I looked everywhere to see what could have made that noise — behind the door, under the carpet,

Under the bed . . .

Behind the curtains . . .

All around the desk . . .

on the bookshelf. But I couldn't find anything unusual. NOT A SINGLE THING!

I thought that maybe I had just imagined the noise. But suddenly . . . there it was again! Stellar Swiss cheese!

Grumble!

And again . . .

Grumble! Grumble!

And then again . . .

Grumble! **Grumble!** *Grumble!*

This time I was **SURE** I had heard something . . . and I realized it was coming from my stomach!

Oh, for the love of cheese — I was cosmically hungry! That's why my stomach was growling.

I needed a quick snack. Some cheese would really hit the spot!

4

I headed toward the refrigerator in my room, but when I opened it, I was in for a terrible surprise. IT WAS EMPTY!

Leaping light-years! This was truly an emErgency.

I didn't have a crumb of cheese rind left! There was only one thing to do. I activated my **wrist phone** and called my sister, Thea.

"Thea, I have a problem. I'm out of cheese!" I exclaimed. "Do you have any STELLAR CHEDDAR? Or maybe a slice of MARTIAN MOZZARELLA? Even some **solar smoked Gouda** would do! I'm

Thea, do you have any stellar cheddar?

Geronimo?

COSMICALLY HUNGRY!"

Right on cue, my poor stomach made the loudest sound yet.

Grumble! Grumble! Grumble!

"Sorry, Geronimo," Thea said. "I finished my last piece of Plutonian Parmesan just a few minutes ago. But why don't you run over to the

Whoa!

SPACE YUM CA

SPACE YUM CAFÉ, Squizzy's restaurant?"

CHEESY COMETS, why didn't I think of that? I thanked Thea for her advice and SCURRIED out the door.

Squizzy was the cook on the *MouseStar 1*, and his restaurant was just a few hallways over from my cabin. I scampered at the *speed of light*, but by the time I turned the last corner, I found myself facing a long line of GROWLING SPACE RODENTS.

That's just not possible!

Hmph!

Grmph!

"That's just **NOT POSSIBLE**!" one grumbled.

"You can't make us all wait!" another joined in.

"I'm extra-galactically hungry!" squeaked a third.

Black holey cheese, what was going on? I turned to the nearest rodent. "Excuse me, why hasn't Squizzy opened the restaurant yet?"

But at that moment, Squizzy appeared in the doorway holding a **big sign** in his claws:

Closed due to a shortage of cheese reserves!

COSMIC CHEESE RAYS!

Squizzy had run out of cheese reserves?! This was a disaster of galactic proportions!

Thinking fast, I ran straight to GALAXY MART, but that was **closed**, too!

Getting desperate, I tried the Cosmic Bakery, the Supernova Grill, and the Planetary Pizza Parlor.

They were all closed — because they had *run out* of cheese!

Was it possible that there wasn't a single cheese rind on the whole spaceship?!

A CHEESE
EMERGENCY!

Starving, I ran to the **control room**, hoping to find my cousin Trap.

Trap **ALWAYS** has a handful of snacks with him . . . and his pockets are **ALWAYS** filled with cheese niblets . . . and he's **ALWAYS** chomping on mouthfuls of cheesy morsels!

But when I found my family in the control room, Trap rushed up to me **desperately**. "Geronimo, did you bring anything to snack on? I ran out of cheese, and I can't find any more!"

Stinky space cheese, what a **mess**! "Actually, I can't find any cheese, either," I replied, whiskers wobbling.

"Well, then this is a real **CHEESE EMERGENCY**!" my cousin squeaked.

At that moment, a cheese-colored hologram* appeared right under my snout. It came from **Hologramix**, our super-sophisticated onboard computer. The hologram repeated, **"Yellow alert! Yellow alert! Yellow alert!"**

* A hologram is a three-dimensional image projected by a light source.

HOLOGRAMIX
MouseStar I's onboard computer

Species: Ultra-advanced artificial intelligence
Specialty: Controls all functions of the spaceship, including the autopilot function
Characteristics: Considers itself to be indispensable
Defining Features: Appears wherever and whenever it's needed

I twisted my tail into a knot. "Hologramix, is this alert because there's no more **cheese** on the spaceship? We have to do something!" I cried.

But Hologramix announced, "Captain, the procurement of that stinky substance which you *mouseoids* call 'cheese' is none of my concern. I have contacted you for more important reasons."

HOLEY CRATERS, how silly I must have seemed! But really, what could be more important than a massive **CHEESE SHORTAGE**? Pacing on my paws, I listened as Hologramix continued.

"A video message has just arrived from an **alien ship** in trouble!" it announced.

Hologramix projected the message from the **TROUBLED** ship on the control room's mega-screen.

Two strange aliens appeared on the screen. They each had *three eyes* and long trunks.

The blue-striped one shook his trunk and said, "**Attention! Attention!** This is an urgent message for all the spaceships traveling in this galaxy. Our ship has **broken down**!"

With tears in all three of his eyes, the other alien begged, "*COME SAVE US!*"

And then, together, they explained, "We are Sergeant Solar and Lieutenant Lunar. We come from the far-off planet of **Flurkon**. We are drifting through space. Please, in the name of stellar brotherhood, **help us**!"

I yelled, "**Holey space cheese!** An alien ship in distress? A call for help? We have to do something!" I gathered my family around. "*Shake a paw*, there's no

time to waste! Locate that ship! We're headed
on an . . .

As Red as Extra-Cheese Pizza Sauce!

In no time, we had tracked down the stranded ship and invited the two aliens aboard the *MouseStar 1*.

As they boarded, I said, "Welcome, interplanetary **friends**! I am Geronimo Stiltonix, captain of this ship. I promise that we will do whatever we can to help you fix —"

Then I was interrupted by my stomach **GRUMBLING**!

My snout turned as red as the sauce on an extra-cheese pizza. How embarrassing!

The taller aLieN waved his trunk and said, "Nice to meet you, Captain. I am

I am Solar . . . . . . and I'm Lunar!

Sergeant **SOLAR**."

"I am Lieutenant **LUNAR**," the other alien added.

And then they said in unison, "We come from the far-off planet of **Flurken**!"

I didn't know whether to look in their RIGHT eyes, their LEFT eyes, or the eyes in the MIDDLE. And was I supposed to shake their paws or their trunks? Oh, **rat-munching robots**, I've never been good at alien manners!

Luckily, **SOLAR** and **LUNAR** kept talking. "We were on an important secret mission for our QUEEN. But now the mission is a failure!"

Suddenly, I heard someone say, "Captain, could I take a look at the engine on the alien ship?"

I turned to see a familiar rodent with curly lilac hair and the most fabumouse smile in all the galaxies. It was **Sally de Wrench**, the official

mechanic aboard our ship. She's the rodent who takes care of the engines and equipment on the **MOUSESTAR 1**.

Sally turned to Solar and Lunar. "Maybe I can **fix** the problem!"

Solar smiled gratefully. "It would be so kind of you to try."

18

Sally headed out to carefully inspect the Flurkonian ship. When she returned, she had **bad news** to share. "I'm sorry, but your ship has a hole in the tank and has lost all of its fuel! The engine runs on a strange substance that I haven't been able to identify. . . ."

As they heard her words, the Flurkonians' six eyes filled with the saddest alien tears I'd ever seen. They sniffled through their trunks and **howled** in unison, "How will we ever return to our beloved planet?"

At that moment, I had an idea that was out of this world! "Don't worry — we'll take you back home. Let's chart a course for planet **Flurkon**!"

THE UNIVERSAL HELPER HOOK

All the best and most advanced interstellar spaceships are equipped with a Universal Helper Hook. They can easily use it to tow other spaceships that are in trouble!

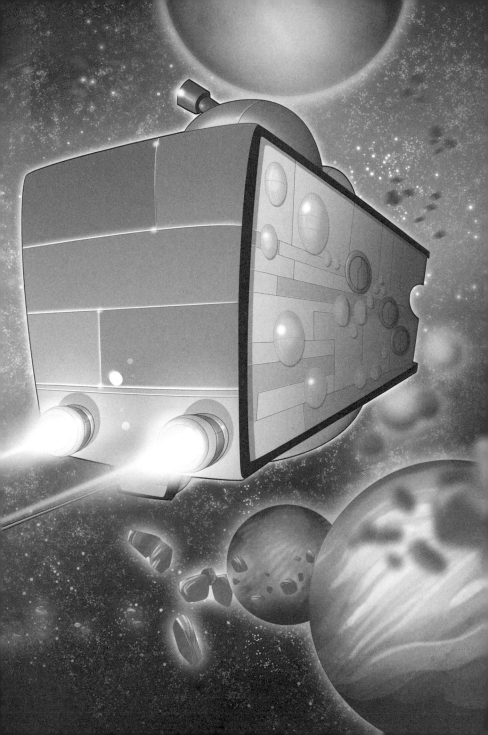

TO PLANET FLURKON!

As we *approached* planet Flurkon, I watched Solar and Lunar carefully. At first, they seemed **happy**, chattering, "It will be so nice to get back home!"

But before long, they began to moan sadly. "Poor us! We will be **thrown** in the flurk. . . ."

"But aren't you happy to **return** to your planet?" I asked, confused.

Together, they replied, "Oh, yes, of course! Flurkon is where our houses, our families, and our friends are. But we do not want to be thrown in the **flurk**!" They both **quaked** as they said the last word.

I asked, "What is the flurk?"

Solar and Lunar each began sobbing uncontrollably. "The flurk is . . . the **TERRIBLE** flurk!" they cried.

Galactic Gorgonzola! I had no idea what they meant, but it sounded horrible!

When we entered planet Flurkon's orbit, I turned to Thea and said, "*QUICK*, prepare the **ship** for landing!"

But just then, Sally intervened. "Captain, this would be a great opportunity to try out the new Teletransportix."

I felt my whiskers **tremble** in fright. I can't stand the words *"try out."* They always mean *"END UP IN TROUBLE"*!

I am a mouse that loves comfort and safety. New things make my **fur stand on end!** But I didn't want Sally and the team to think I was a 'fraidy mouse. What kind of captain

would I be then? So I said, "Of course —
let's try it!"

In two shakes of a mouse's tail, I got on
the **Teletransportix** platform with
Sergeant Solar and Lieutenant Lunar. We
were ready to depart for Flurkon when Thea
HURRIED IN and said, "Geronimo,
I'm coming, too! I want to take some
pictures of the alien planet for
my new album, *Images of the
Galaxies*."

I'm coming, too!

Then Trap appeared on
the platform. "Geronimo,
I'm coming, too! I want
to taste all the **alien
recipes** for my TV
show, *Space Bites*!"

Then **PROFESSOR
GREENFUR**, the

MouseStar 1's senior scientist, ran up and said, "I'm coming, too! I want to study the strange alien fuel and the vegetation of planet Flurkon."

Finally, my nephew Benjamin and his friend Bugsy Wugsy appeared, looking timid.

Benjamin said: "Uncle, we have to do some research on foreign planets for school. Can we come, too? Please? We'll be *so good*! We'll do everything you say!"

Cheese and crackers, I couldn't bring myself to say no! So with no time to waste, we all gathered on the platform of the **Teletransportix**.

From the Encyclopedia Galactica
THE TELETRANSPORTIX

The Teletransportix is a fabumouse piece of technology! It's capable of dematerializing molecules, teletransporting them, and then making them rematerialize anywhere. You might find yourself far, far away before you even wiggle your whiskers!

Very rarely, something gets lost in the transference of molecules, like a random whisker or the tip of a tail. Squeak!

We're ready, too!

Teletransportix ready!

AT MOST, YOU'LL LOSE A WHISKER OR TWO!

Sally placed herself at the **control panel**. She explained, "Your molecules will be broken up into minuscule particles, which will be transferred by the Teletransportix to the alien planet. They should REMATERIALIZE there exactly as they are now —"

My fur stood on end. "Wait! What do you mean they '*should*'?"

Sally smoothed her hair and said nonchalantly, "Don't worry, Captain, I am practically almost SURE this will work!"

Cosmic cheese chunks! I had to ask,

"Are you **sure**, or only *practically almost* sure?"

Sally thought for a moment. "Well, the MOLECULES are small, and you're traveling a long distance. There could be a small dispersion of cells. But at most, you'll lose a whisker or two!"

I yelped. "Mousey meteorites! I care about my cells . . . and my whiskers, too!"

Sally rolled her eyes. "Captain, do you want to get to the alien planet? Yes or no?"

"Well, yes," I said, "but —"

Sally didn't give me time to finish. "Good! Then get on the platform." When we were all in position, she pressed a series of buttons and asked confidently, "Are you ready to get Teletransportixed?"

Oh, green cheesy moons, I DIDN'T FeeL ReaDY!

That's because:

First: I had never teletransported before!

Second: The idea of my cells dispersing was fur-raising to even think about!

Third: I wanted to keep all of my whiskers!

But since I'm the captain of this ship, I have to lead by example. So I responded, "Um . . . I'm ready!"

The others all echoed, "We're ready!"

Immediately, I felt a strange tingling in my tail . . .

And a strange CHILL down my back . . .

And a strange spinning in my head . . .

I felt shaken up like a Martian mozzarella milkshake!

When I opened my eyes . . . we were on the

alien planet!

The first thing that I noticed was a giant **volcano** towering nearby. It was erupting with **thick yellow lava**! Everywhere else, there were green fields covered with strange plants.

A group of aliens similar to **SOLAR** and **LUNAR** approached us. They had the same floppy ears, long trunks, and three **EYES** each.

In the middle of the group, I could see an alien wearing a **GOLDEN** crown with a beautiful

Huh?

Whoa!

Aaahhhh!

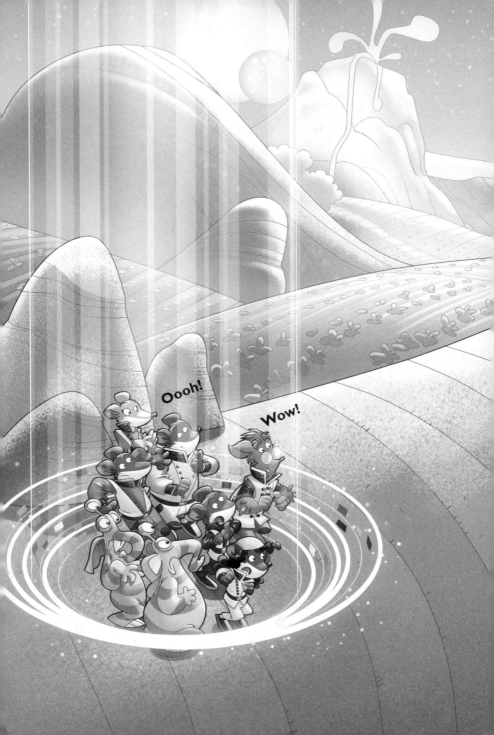

emerald stone in the center. In her right hand, she held a golden scepter topped with another green stone.

Solar STAMMERED, frightened, "Th-th-that is our queen."

And Lunar added in a whisper, "Queen Stella."

They both began to shake like chattering cheddar. "She's going to have us thrown in the **flurk**!"

The queen did have a very serious expression on her face. She approached with great strides, glaring at poor Solar and Lunar with her three enormouse eyes. The two aliens fell to their knees before her.

"Have you carried out your *secret mission*?" the queen asked.

Solar and Lunar didn't dare raise their six eyes. With lowered trunks, they muttered, "Umm . . . we're afraid not. The ship ran out of fuel! Please, Your Highness, don't have us thrown in the flurk!"

The queen was **furious**! She snapped, "I knew you were fools! You don't want to be thrown in the **flurk**? Well, that is *exactly* what happens to those who don't complete their secret missions!"

I didn't know **what to do**. I knew I shouldn't stick my snout where it didn't belong, but I also didn't want poor **SOLAR** and **LUNAR** to be thrown in the Flurk — whatever that meant! It really gets my tail in a twist when someone is **PUNISHED** for no reason.

As politely as I could, I said, "Your Highness, allow me to introduce myself. My name is Stiltonix, **Geronimo Stiltonix**.

You fools!

Sigh!

Sob!

I am the captain of the *MouseStar 1*, home of the spacemice! I have a **special** request to ask of you."

Queen Stella turned to me with her three big eyes and her long eyelashes and . . . smiled!

How Lucky for Me!

Stella **FLAPPED** her left ear like a fan. Then she put an arm around my shoulders and said, "My, what a handsome captain! So, Gerry — I can call you Gerry, right?"

Even though I hate nicknames, I replied, "Of course, *Your Highness*."

"You're so cute, Gerry!" she gushed. "Tell me, are you . . . **married**?"

"Um . . . no," I said cautiously.

The queen batted her eyelashes, twisted her trunk into a heart shape, and **giggled**. "Good! *How lucky for me*. . . ."

Cosmic cheese rays, how **humiliating**! I tried to pretend that nothing unusual was happening, so I cleared my throat and said, "Your Highness, I beg you to **forgive** Sergeant Solar and Lieutenant Lunar."

Stella distractedly fanned her **ears** and sighed. She didn't seem very interested in Solar and Lunar at all! She stared at me with her three **eyes**.

(I didn't even know which eye to look at!)

The way the queen was staring gave me a squeaking **suspicion** that she was very interested in . . . **me**!

"Listen, my brave and handsome space captain, I don't understand why you are so interested in these two *fools*," Queen Stella said. "Solar and Lunar should be thrown in the flurk! But since you are so *cute*, I've decided to forgive them. However, I am only doing it because *you* asked me to!"

Hearing her words, Solar and Lunar both breathed a *sigh* of relief and finally smiled.

They whispered to me gratefully, "Thanks, **Captain Stiltonix**. We owe you!"

I didn't have time to respond, because just then **Stella** grabbed me with her trunk and took my paw.

Oh, stinky space cheese, my worst fears were true! The queen had fallen in love with me!

In a voice as sweet as *Gorgonzola and honey*, she said, "So, handsome captain, would you like to take a stroll with me? I'll give you a tour of my beautiful planet. I'm sure you will **like** it so much that you won't want to leave!"

I wanted to **RUN AWAY** as fast as my paws would take me! "Thank you, Your Highness," I said politely, instead. "I'm sure that planet Flurkon is very beautiful, but we need to return to our **spaceship** now."

Stella's middle eye opened **wide** in shock.

"What's that? You want to leave already? Not a chance, Captain!" she cried. "I will organize a nice **banquet** in your honor, and you will **see** my castle, and then you will ask me to **marry you**, and then

we'll see what happens!"

Squeak!

I muttered, "And if not . . . ?"

"Then I will throw all of you in the **flurk**!" the queen declared. "But that won't be necessary, right, Gerry?" She batted her lashes again. "After all, I'm sure you have never seen three eyes as *beautiful* as mine. . . ."

What an **intergalactic nightmare**!

A Familiar Scent...

I was already REGRETTING bringing Benjamin and Bugsy to planet Flurkon with us. What if the queen decided to throw us **all** in the flurk?

"Geronimo, the banquet idea isn't a bad one!" Trap whispered to me.

My cousin is always thinking about food! But it was true — we hadn't had anything to eat in what felt like light-years....

Thea added, "We need time to make an ESCAPE PLAN!"

So we followed the queen to the royal palace for the banquet. She didn't take her eyes off me the whole way. **Not one of them**!

The royal palace was at

the top of a hill, surrounded by fields. It was a strange yellow color and smelled **familiar**, though I couldn't figure out why.

Stella took me on a tour of the plants in the fields, exclaiming proudly, "Look at how the **goober** plants have grown this year! In the summer, we always organize a Goober Festival. We sing, we dance, and best of all, we eat **goobers** that have just been picked. You like goobers, right, Captain?"

I tried to be as polite as possible, even though alien food made my whiskers wobble. "Goobers? Um, actually, I've never tasted them, but I would be **willing to try**!"

Stella widened her eyes in shock. "You've *never* tasted goobers?"

Turning to the aliens behind her, she said,

"Did you hear that? Gerry has never tasted **goobers**! Isn't that funny?"

To please her, the aliens of the court all laughed. "Very, very funny, Your Highness!"

There was one alien who didn't laugh. He seemed **important**, because he carried a large staff. He was tall and muscular, and his three eyes **STARED** at me with a troubling expression. Cheesy comets, he was intimidating!

But the queen didn't notice. She only had eyes for me!

Stella giggled and tugged on my paw. "You're so sweet, Gerry. Even if you've never tasted **goobers**, I adore you anyway! But you'll like them, I'm sure. We Flurkonians don't eat anything else!"

To be polite, I responded, "Um, of course

I'll like them. You know, it's actually been a while since I ate —"

At that moment, my stomach grumbled!

Grumble! **Grumble!** *Grumble!*

Oh, for all of Saturn's rings, how embarrassing!

But Stella just laughed, shaking her trunk. "Listen to my sweet captain's empty stomach! Don't worry, soon we'll have all the goobers we can eat."

I wasn't sure if that made my stomach feel any better.

Thea whispered in my ear, "The **queen** has quite a crush on you!"

And Trap muttered, "I really don't understand what she sees in you, Cousin . . . after all, I'm much better looking!"

I would have traded places with Trap at the **SPEED OF LIGHT**!

Just then, Professor Greenfur whispered, "Captain, I have done some analysis on the goober plants, and —"

But before he could finish, Queen **Stella** trumpeted loudly, *"So, Gerry, do you like my castle?"*

I peered up at the beautiful yellow castle, complete with a drawbridge and many **FLAGS** waving atop the towers. It smelled awfully familiar, but I just couldn't put my paw on why. . . .

I WANT TO GO BACK TO MY SPACESHIP!

When we entered the castle, we were led to the banquet hall. Swiss-munching spacemice, it was awfully *glitzy*! There was a long table, tall columns, **enormouse** sculptures, beautiful artwork, giant mirrors, and painted ceilings.

But everything seemed to be made of the same **strange** material as the castle. It was a yellow substance, like . . . **cheese**!

Stella batted her eyelashes and playfully mussed my fur.

"*My dear Gerry*, would you wait here for one minute? I want to go tell the cook that this special goober banquet has to be the **best ever**!" She squeezed my paw. "But don't worry. While I'm gone, my **GRAND ADVISOR** will keep you company!"

With that, she yelled, "Nova, I order you to keep my beautiful cosmic captain and his friends company. I will return right away!"

Nova, the grand advisor, was the **tall** and **muscular** alien who had been glaring at me earlier. Oh, for the love of all things cheesy, this was just my luck!

Nova's three **eyes** all glared at me suspiciously. But he bowed to the **queen** and responded, "Of course, beloved Queen Stella. Your wish is my command!"

I couldn't wait for the queen to leave so we could organize our escape. I wanted to

return to the **MOUSESTAR 1** in two shakes of a mouse's tail!

When she'd disappeared, I asked Thea under my breath, "Psst! Does your **wrist phone** work? Tell Sally to Teletransportix us back to the ship as soon as possible!"

Thea shook her head. "We've lost communications with the **spaceship**. There's some strange interference on this planet, but I'll keep trying!"

"Be careful not to get caught!" I responded, turning as white as mozzarella. "Otherwise they'll throw us all in the **flurk** . . . whatever that means!"

Then I quietly turned to **GREENFUR** and asked, "Are goobers okay for rodents to eat?"

Looking down at a leaf in his paw, Greenfur responded, "I am **ANALYZING** the goober plants, Captain! But I haven't finished yet. . . ."

I nodded and then looked at Trap. "Try to find out what this castle is made of. It has a **strange smell**!"

And finally, I turned to Benjamin and Bugsy and gave them a reassuring SMiLE. "Get ready! Soon we'll all be on our way back to the *MouseStar 1*!"

Are goobers okay to eat?

IT'S ALL MADE OF FLURK!

A few moments later, I felt something ruffle my fur. I jumped!

When I turned around, Stella was back. "Hello, handsome! You're an awfully good-looking rodent. Now if only your ears weren't so small . . . and your nose wasn't so short . . . but I like you anyway!"

I blushed in embarrassment. I hate being the center of attention!

The queen laughed and sat down at the head of the table. "Compliments make you blush, eh, Captain? How adorable! Come sit next to me, in the grand advisor's seat. Nova can sit on the other side."

She waved a hand, shooing the advisor away.

Nova's face clouded over with **anger**. The queen didn't even *look* at him, and she motioned ME to his seat!

But instead of having an outburst, the grand advisor bowed and responded, "Of course, Your Highness. Your wish is my command!"

Grrrr!

Stella smiled with satisfaction as I sat next to her. "My handsome captain, now you will taste the best of Flurkonian cooking!"

As aliens brought in plates piled high

GOOBER SOUP

GOOBER ROAST

GOOBER STRUDEL

GOOBER CAKE

CANDIED GOOBERS

with food, Stella rattled off the menu proudly. "We'll start with appetizers made from **goober** butter, then **goober** soup with **goober** toast, **goober** meatloaf, **goober** roast, and finally a **goober** strudel, **goober** cake, and candied **goobers**!"

As she spoke, I looked over at Trap, who was **sniffing** his plate, his glass, and even the table and chair.

HOW STRANGE! It was almost as if he wanted to eat them. Curious, I looked more closely at my plate. Black holey galaxies! It looked like it was made of . . . **cheese**!

I sniffed it, and it also really smelled just like . . . **cheese**!

I was about to sink my teeth in, just to check, when Stella yelped, "What are you doing, Gerry? Don't tell me you want to **eat** the plate! How rude! You don't eat that — the plate is made of flurk!"

Flurk was . . .

. . . **cheese** ?!

I asked hesitantly, "Your Highness, forgive my ignorance, but . . . **what is flurk?**"

Stella began to laugh and laugh, her trunk bouncing with amusement. "*Ha, ha, ha!*"

All the other aliens followed her lead and began to laugh, too. "*Ha, ha, ha!*" The whole banquet hall echoed with laughter!

The only one who didn't laugh was Nova.

HA HA
HA

Maybe he was still **OFFENDED** because I was sitting in his seat. I was sure he was giving me an **EVIL** glare. Starry space dust, I didn't want to be on his bad side!

HA HA
HA

Stella and the aliens of the court laughed until they *cried*. Then the queen dried all three of her eyes with different tissues and ordered,

HAH
HA

HAHAHA

Huh?

Hmmm . . .

HA HA
HA

"That's enough!"

The court immediately fell silent.

The queen gave me an affectionate pat with her trunk and said, "Dear Gerry, you're so *Funny*! We Flurkonians love those who make us laugh."

Then she called for **SOLAR** and **LUNAR**. "Since I saved your lives, make

HA HA HA

HA HA HA

yourselves useful and explain to my foreign **sweetheart** what flurk is!"

Solar said, "Flurk is yellow."

"Flurk comes from the **volcano**," Lunar added.

And together they explained, "The boiling flurk from the volcano is poured into the tanks of our **spaceships** as fuel."

"But when flurk gets cold," Solar said, "it becomes really **hard**. Then we use it to make houses — and everything else!"

"The palace is made of **flurk**!" Lunar exclaimed.

"The plates and the glasses and chairs and tables are made of **flurk**!" Solar went on.

Together, they finished, "Everything is made of **flurk**!"

At that very moment, something terrible happened.

Trap stood up and squeaked, "Leaping light-years, this is **cheese**!"

And then my cousin nibbled on a plate!

Stella and all the aliens of the court watched him, completely **scandalized**. Crusty space cheese! The only one who snickered was Nova.

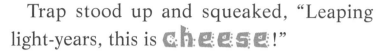

From the Encyclopedia Galactica
OUTER SPACE ETIQUETTE

Strict table manners should be observed when visiting unfamiliar planets. These include not nibbling on furniture and other objects, not blowing your nose in your napkin, and not squeaking with your mouth full!

Yum!

A Flurk-Flavored Mess!

Stella stood up, **FURIOUS**. She swirled her golden scepter in the air and hollered, "The stranger in the yellow suit has deeply offended us! Take him to the volcano and throw him in the boiling **flurk** — at once!"

Holey craters, what a mess! They were going to throw Trap in the **volcano**!

"Your Highness, forgive him!" I squeaked, trying to make things right. "My cousin is just confused. . . ."

Stella looked at Trap, then at me, then back at Trap again. "Your cousin, you say?" she asked. "You don't look alike **at all**!"

I begged, "Please, Your Highness, don't throw him in the flurk! My cousin nibbled on your plate because, where we come from, cheese — I mean flurk — is for eating!"

Stella chuckled in disbelief. "You eat flurk? You are awfully strange. . . ."

I replied diplomatically, "Yes, we eat flurk, but it's because we aren't fortunate enough to have any goobers!"

The queen smiled at that. "My poor captain, forced to eat flurk! Here, taste this appetizer covered in goober butter." She took a cracker topped with a brownish cream and put it in my mouth.

OH, FOR ALL THE LUNAR CHEESE IN THE GALAXY, I was eating alien food — and I didn't even know what it was!

1.

I could only hope:

1. That the goobers didn't make me break out in BLISTERS!

2. That they didn't make me grow a **trunk**!

2.

3. That they didn't turn me **blue**!

I chewed slowly. . . . I was **worried**!

Then I swallowed and waited to see what horrible effects the goobers would have. . . . I was **really worried**!

3.

And you know what?

The goober-covered cracker was really **good**! It tasted like peanut butter!

Thea leaned over and whispered, "Don't worry, Geronimo. GREENFUR analyzed the plants and concluded that **goobers are actually ... peanuts**!"

I was so relieved I could hardly squeak! But then I noticed that Stella was staring at me, waiting for my reaction. So I said, "This goober butter is delicious!"

Stella breathed a big sigh of relief. "Good thing you like **goobers**! If you'd told me that you wanted to eat the flurk instead, I would have had to throw you in the volcano. And that would have been a shame — *you're so cute*! So you're all forgiven, but your cousin had better not nibble on any more plates. He's ruining my formal dinnerware!"

With a sigh of relief, we dug into the other dishes. It was a fabumouse banquet! The goober *specialties* were yummy,

even if they were surrounded by all that **cheese**. Not being able to taste it was a terrible temptation!

Toward the end of the meal, I noticed that Trap looked **guilty**.

Immediately, my fur stood on end. Holey craters, what had he done now? Had he gotten into more **trouble**?

A waiter ran to the queen and whispered something in her ear.

Stella glared at Trap with all three of her eyes. She looked **FURIOUS**!

She cried, "Throw that foreigner in the yellow suit into the boiling flurk!"

My worst fears had come true: Trap had nibbled on the leg of the table. Celestial cheddar, now we were all in big trouble!

I had to think fast, so I said, "Your Highness, you must excuse him. For us rodents, cheese — um, I mean flurk — is an irresistible temptation! Trap is a very gluttonous mouse. When he sees flurk, he can't *control himself*. . . ."

Trap nodded. "It's true!"

It was true, all right!

Just then, I had a fabumouse idea. "If you forgive him, Your Highness, my cousin will perform a **magic** act for you!" I gave Trap a look. "Right, Cousin? You're an **amazing** magician!"

"The best in all the galaxies,

Your Majesty!" Trap proudly gloated.

The room was silent while the queen thought hard. Cosmic cheese dust, would she agree? Finally, she nodded. "Let's see this magic act!"

STARDUST AND CHEDDAR UNDER YOUR NOSE . . .

Trap pulled his cosmic magician's ultra-tiny portable magic kit out of his pocket, muttering, "I knew this would come in handy sooner or later!"

He put on his foldable **top hat**, **cape**, and **gloves**, and grabbed his **wand**. Then he **jumped** up on a table as if it were a stage!

"My dear Flurkonians, my name is **Trap Stiltonix**, Galactic Magician!" He waved his **cape** with a flourish. "Today, you will be the lucky audience for some **grand magic!**"

The aliens of the court seemed very interested. Even Stella watched attentively with all three **eyes**.

Trap announced, "First, I will make this goober pie disappear!"

With that, he slipped the **goober pie** into his hat. Then he flipped the hat over and . . . the pie was gone!

The aliens of the court all exclaimed in unison, "**Oooohhhh!**"

"Look in my hat," Trap said proudly. "It's empty — **completely empty!**"

Stella ordered, "Nova, check to see if it's really empty. The goober pie must have gone **somewhere!**"

Nova seemed annoyed, but he got up to

check as the queen requested. "The hat is **empty**, Your Majesty."

The other aliens of the court all got up to check, too. "It's **completely empty**!" they reported in awe.

Trap grinned in satisfaction.

"You see, ladies and gentlemen? This is not a scam, just authentic **cosmic magic**!

It's completely empty!

Your Majesty, see for yourself!" He stood in front of Stella. Right under her trunk, he **tapped** the hat with his wand three times. . . .

Tap! Tap! Tap!

Then he solemnly pronounced the magic words, "Stardust and cheddar under your nose. For you, my dear, a lovely . . . rose!"

A beautiful yellow rose appeared in Trap's paw, which he offered to the **queen** with a bow.

Stella applauded wildly. "Amazing! Well done!"

I breathed a sigh of relief. My cousin was really behaving himself!

"Magician, I order you to do more **magic**!"

Stella said. "Make something else disappear!"

The aliens behind her all **cheered**. They wanted to see more magic, too!

The only one who didn't say anything was Nova. He was glowering in a corner! I couldn't help wondering if he was **plotting** something. . . .

Hearing the cheers, Trap grinned and twirled his tail. What tricks did he have up his sleeve now?

He cleared his throat and solemnly announced, "For this next magic trick, I need something **very valuable**. Your Majesty, would you give me your **crown**?"

Stella's three eyes widened in **surprise**. She didn't want to take off her crown! But she was clearly **AS CURIOUS AS**

A SPACECAT to see what kind of magic Trap would perform with it.

Finally, after a moment, she handed over the crown. "Magician, I advise you to take good care of it. Otherwise I will throw you in the **flurk**!"

"Don't worry, Your Majesty!" Trap reassured her, placing the crown carefully in his hat. "Watch!"

Before

After

Tap! Tap! Tap!

As soon as he'd finished tapping it, Trap spun the top hat and . . . the crown had disappeared!

The queen didn't **applaud** like she had the first time.

Rats! I had a bad feeling about this.

Stella barked, "Okay, magician, you made it disappear. Now give it back!"

Trap confidently tapped his wand on the hat and said, "Here, Your Majesty, your crown is in the hat — look!"

Stella looked. She looked again. Then she looked once more.

78

Then she yelled, "It's not here! My crown is *gone!*"

Martian mozzarella, I hoped it wasn't true! I looked in the hat, too. **IT REALLY WASN'T THERE!**

The hat was **empty**!

The queen cried, "No more jokes, magician. Give me back my crown!"

Trap looked around, flustered. "I — I don't understand," he stammered. "I hid it under the table, but — it's not there!"

Oh, for all the planets in the solar system! Trap had lost the queen's crown!

Stella stood up, jabbed her golden scepter in the air, and proclaimed, "**LOCK** the foreigners in the prison! Until they give me the **crown**, they aren't going anywhere!"

"Your Majesty, there must be some mistake,"

I said, trying to calm her down. "Let's look for it carefully. Maybe the CROWN rolled into a corner!"

Stella frowned. "My handsome captain, I like you — but if we don't find my crown, you rodents will all be thrown in the flurk!"

Galactic Gorgonzola! The very idea made me tremble from the edges of my ears to the tip of my tail!

"We're not thieves — mouse's honor," I insisted, hoping she'd believe me.

At that moment, Nova approached. My fur stood on end.

"Your Majesty, I bet Captain Gerry hid the crown!" Nova said. "He could have done it while his cousin was distracting you."

"That's a lie!" I squeaked.

Stella seemed confused. She didn't know

whether to believe me or her grand advisor.

So she shook her ears, stretched her **trunk**, and declared, "I want to believe Gerry the cute captain, but Nova is my grand advisor! So I **ORDER** . . ."

What would she order? My whiskers were shaking from the stress!

Stella **finally** concluded, "I order Grand Advisor Nova and Captain Gerry to **COMPETE** in a game of golf!"

I didn't even have time to squeak before the queen added, "The winner will take me as his bride, and the loser . . . will be **thrown** in the flurk!"

Celestial cheddar, this was getting **worse and worse**!

Stella turned to leave, waving a hand and commanding, "Sergeant **SOLAR** and Lieutenant **LUNAR**, make yourselves useful and escort the foreigners to the castle prison!"

Then she gave me a little smile. "I'm sorry, **my wonderfully whiskered captain**. You may end up in the flurk, after all . . . unless you can beat Nova tomorrow! Of course, he is our planetary **GOLF** champion."

It's decided!

Gulp!

Champion? Oh, for the love of all things cheesy, this was a disaster!

"But maybe you're good, too!" the queen said hopefully. "Are you good at golf, Gerry?"

I was not good . . . not good at all!

Oh, why had I ended up on this alien planet? I am not a very courageous mouse! This was all much too fur-raising for a 'fraidy mouse like me.

Stella headed out the door. "I'm going to prepare for the wedding," she called over her shoulder. "Tomorrow I will be married! Who will the lucky groom be?"

My stomach churned like spoiled cheddar chowder as we were escorted to the prison.

WE WILL BE AS SLY AS SPACECATS, UNCLE!

Sergeant Solar and Lieutenant Lunar led us to the prison in the **dungeon** of the royal palace. As we walked, we realized that the whole castle was made of flurk, including the prison.

It was a cheese prison!

As they locked us in, Solar and Lunar whispered, "We're so sorry to do this, especially after you saved us when the **queen** wanted to throw us in the flurk!"

I sighed and patted Lunar on the hand. "It's not your fault. You're just following orders."

Once they'd left, I asked Thea, "Were

you able to contact Sally? If she can reach us with the Teletransportix now, we'll be SAVED!"

Thea raised an eyebrow. "I have **GOOD** news and **BAD** news. . . ."

Bad news is the last thing you want to hear when you're a prisoner on an **alien planet**!

"The bad news is that it is impossible to communicate with the *MouseStar 1*," Thea went on calmly.

I yelped, "IMPOSSIBLE? Cosmic cheese chunks, that's **HORRIBLE**! What's the good news?"

"The good news is that I made an agreement with Sally before we left," Thea said. "If she doesn't hear from us, she'll automatically Teletransportix us to the spaceship in EXACTLY . . ." She stopped to look at her watch. "Twenty-four hours, twenty-four minutes, and twenty-four stellar seconds from now!"

"OH, FOR ALL THE SHOOTING STARS!" I cried, trying not to tear out my whiskers. "In twenty-four hours, we'll already have been thrown in the flurk!"

I didn't lose it!

I spun to face Trap. This was all his fault! "Where did you lose the crown?"

Trap looked offended. "I didn't lose it," he grumbled. "I'm a **professional magician**! One of the aliens must have grabbed it from right under my snout!"

Could that be true?

I thought for a moment, then muttered, "If only we could get out of this **prison** and look for the crown."

Professor Greenfur cleared his throat. "Captain, I've analyzed the makeup of this prison cell," he announced. "It is, in fact, pure cheese!"

Trap mumbled, "Tell us something we **don't** know. . . ."

Greenfur ignored Trap and continued, "According to my calculations, the walls are **7,303,746,352,959** decimeters thick. To dig a tunnel big enough for all of us to get through, six mice would have to eat for at least . . . twenty-eight **hours**!"

My whiskers drooped. "But we don't have twenty-eight **hours**!" I cried, pacing the floor. "Tomorrow morning I'll lose the golf game, and we'll all be thrown in the flurk!

Crusty space cheese, I don't want to turn into mouse fondue!"

Greenfur piped up again. "Captain, I'm sorry to contradict you, but —"

"But what?" I yelped. Was there hope?

Greenfur explained, "According to my calculations, if we dug a smaller tunnel, we could actually do it in . . . four hours, maximum!"

I twisted my tail, perplexed. "Okay, but what will we be able to do with a smaller TUNNEL?" I asked. "If we can't get through, it's useless!"

Just then, Benjamin tugged on my sleeve. "Bugsy and I are small, Uncle Geronimo. We can escape through the tunnel and look for the crown!"

I squeaked, "Send two mouselings off by

From the Encyclopedia Galactica
THE SLY SPACECAT

The sly spacecat is a unique feline — he has six paws! He moves quickly and quietly, and is known for his sneaky ability to move around undetected.

themselves on a dangerous alien planet? **Absolutely not!**"

But Benjamin and Bugsy insisted. "We beg you, Uncle, we'll be **careful**! We won't be spotted. We'll be as invisible as remote galaxies, as elusive as comets, and as sly as SPACECATS!"

Trap nudged me. "Benjamin and Bugsy are right, Geronimo. *Let them go!*"

"They're our only hope," Thea agreed.

"I have something to help them," Greenfur added. "During dinner I made a mAp of the castle, just in case we needed it!" He held up a detailed map in one paw.

Benjamin and Bugsy grinned and looked up at me with wide eyes. **Cheese and crackers**, what choice did I have? I had to say **yes**!

IF ONLY GRANDFATHER
WILLIAM WERE HERE. . . .

We all ate away at the wall of the prison
for hours and hours. It was easy — we were
munching on delicious cheese! It was
a good thing we were all so hungry.

Once the tunnel was finished, we said
good-bye to Benjamin and Bugsy. "*HURRY!*"
I said. "But be careful — don't get caught!"

Benjamin hugged me. "Don't worry about
us, Uncle." He waved as they disappeared. It
was cosmically hard to watch them go!

We piled our blankets in Benjamin's and
Bugsy's beds to make it look like they were
sleeping, in case anyone came to check on us.

I spent the night pacing the prison floor

on my paws. The next morning, Sergeant **SOLAR** and Lieutenant **LUNAR** opened the door.

They announced together, "By order of the

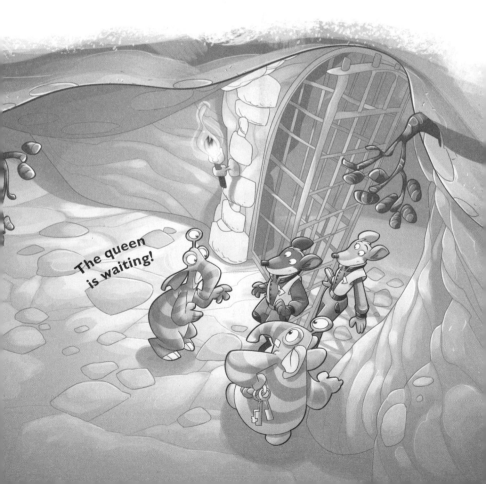

queen, we must lead **Captain Gerry** to the golf course!"

Immediately, Thea jumped up and said, "I'm coming, too — I'm his caddy*!"

I looked at her, surprised, but she didn't give me time to squeak. "You need a caddy, right, Geronimo?"

I nodded, playing along. "Um, of course! I absolutely do! I can't possibly play golf without a caddy."

Solar and Lunar looked at each other uncertainly, then nodded and responded in unison. "It's true — every self-respecting GOLFER has his own caddy!" With that, they led me and Thea out of the prison.

When we arrived at the golf course, a crowd of aliens had gathered. They chattered excitedly, curious to see who was going to win the queen's hand in marriage!

* A caddy helps a golfer by carrying his clubs.

STARRY SPACE DUST! How had I gotten myself into such a massive mess?

I am really not an athletic mouse — I've always wanted to be a *writer*!

I nibbled my paw-nails and said to Thea under my breath, "I'm no good at playing golf! If only Grandfather William Stiltonix were here — he's fabumouse at golf. Maybe he would be able to give me some tips!"

My sister smiled and winked. "Don't worry, Geronimo. I have a **surprise** for you!"

I'M ENORMOUSELY BAD AT GOLF!

The golf game on planet Flurkon was just like the one I knew . . . but the ball was made of **flurk**!

And the clubs were made of **flurk**!

And the flagpole was made of **flurk**!

The only thing **not** made of flurk was the grass and the **goober** plants! Goober plants were growing everywhere along the course.

Thwack!

Nova shot first. His ball landed just a few inches from the **hole**. My ball, on the other hand, landed in a **sand trap**. Just my luck!

Nova finished the hole in two shots. Cheesy comets, he was good!

I, on the other hand, wasted eleven shots getting out of the sand . . . then I used twelve more to get close to the flag . . . and finally thirteen more to get the ball in the hole!

I'm enormously bad at golf!

Who was I kidding? I was **never** going to win this game! We were **doomed**!

Why wasn't my grandfather there? He would know exactly what to do.

At that moment, a voice that I had known since I was a young mouselet called out, "Grandson, quit 𝖒𝖔𝖕𝖎𝖓𝖌 and show them that you're a stellar captain! You need to win this game and save your 𝕋𝔼𝔸𝕄!"

I could have 𝕾𝕼𝖀𝕰𝕬𝕶𝕰𝕯 𝖂𝕴𝕿𝕳 𝕵𝕺𝖄!

Grandson, quit moping!

It was him — Grandfather William! But how was that possible? He hadn't come to planet Flurkon with us!

I whirled around and said, "Grandfather, is it really you?"

But my grandfather was nowhere to be seen. The only mouse there was Thea — and she was **smiling**!

"I had a feeling that you would need **Grandfather**!" she said. "So I came prepared to say everything he would usually say!"

I was cosmically confused. "But how can you **imitate** his voice so well?" I asked. "You really sounded like him!"

Thea winked and showed me a small device that looked like a **microphone**. "This is the super-micro voice imitator that Trap loaned me. He uses it in his **magic shows**!"

Using Grandfather William's voice, she hollered, "Geronimo! You're not bending your **paws** enough! Your head is too high! Your grip isn't firm enough! And your tail is **crooked**!"

I don't know how, but . . . **it worked!**

With my grandfather's advice (or, should I say, Thea's advice), I began to play better! **Hole** after **hole**, I caught up more and more. By the last hole, Nova and I were **tied!**

Finally, the game was almost over. We were both near the flag. The many **eyes** of all the aliens in the court were on us.

Nova fanned his ears, took a deep breath, and hit the ball.

I saw it roll toward the flag, almost in **slow motion**, until . . . it went in the hole!

Nova stood up straight, **satisfied**. He looked at me with all three eyes as if to say, "Let's see if you can do better!"

My knees were **knocking** . . .

My paws were **sweating** . . .

And my whiskers **wobbled** in fright!

But then I heard my grandfather's voice yelling, "Grandson, I order you to put the ball in the hole! Think about Benjamin and Bugsy! **Do not let me down**, or you won't be worthy of the name **Stiltonix**!"

I lined up my shot and took careful aim, but right before I swung . . . Nova **tripped** me! And the queen didn't even see it. I **messed** up my shot!

I had **lost**! We would be thrown in the flurk!

Stella held one of Nova's arms in the air. "Here is the winner!"

Nova proudly waved his ears. His three eyes shone with **triumph**!

The queen approached me, shaking her head sadly. "You're so cute, I'm sorry to throw you in the **flurk** . . . but it's been decided!"

Ohhh!

She turned to her guards. *"SEIZE HIM!"*

The crowd rejoiced — everyone but Solar and Lunar, the only *aliens* on the whole planet who didn't want to see us get thrown in the bubbling, flurk-filled volcano.

A Wedding on the Horizon!

It was finally happening. My worst **nightmare** — we were about to be thrown in the flurk! I saw the melted cheese **boiling** in the crater below me, and I squeezed my eyes shut tight. But suddenly, Benjamin and Bugsy appeared! Luckily, no one had discovered that they were missing yet.

"**STOP, EVERYONE!**" Benjamin yelled. "We found the crown!"

Cosmic cheese niblets, could it be true? I *turned around*.

Trap, Thea, and Professor Greenfur *turned around*.

Stella, Nova, and all the aliens of the court
turned around.

It was true — Benjamin was holding the
queen's crown in his hand! We
were saved!

Stella yelped, "My crown! Where did you
find it?"

Benjamin frowned. "It was hidden under
Grand Advisor **Nova's** desk."

Ohhhh!

Here's your crown!

All three of Stella's eyes grew wide. She seemed surprised — VERY SURPRISED.

She turned to her grand advisor in disbelief. "Nova, is this true?"

Nova's face turned a **dark blue** in embarrassment . . .

Then it turned a deep **turquoise** in shame . . .

Then **light blue** in fear . . .

Finally, he hung his head and mumbled, "It's true, Your Majesty."

I couldn't believe my ears!

Stella shook her trunk in *astonishment.* "Nova, why would you do such a thing?"

Nova lowered all three of his eyes and confessed quietly, "I did it . . . because *I love you!* I have *always* loved you!"

Green cheesy moons, I never saw that coming!

Nova went on, blushing. "Your three eyes sparkle like a supernova*, your trunk is as *willowy* as a comet's tail, and your skin shines brighter than a *star!*"

Stella's face lit up. "How romantic! But I still don't understand why you **stole** my crown."

"Your Majesty, you wanted to marry Captain Gerry," Nova responded, embarrassed. "I was jealous!"

Stella *tenderly* put her trunk around

---

* A supernova is a star that suddenly becomes extremely bright because of a huge explosion within it.

his shoulders. "My dear grand advisor, why didn't you ever confess your love?"

Nova shrugged. "Because I'm . . .

!"

"How cute is that?" Stella laughed and batted her eyelashes. "I had a secret admirer and I didn't even know it!"

Just then, Nova took a **deep breath**, knelt down, and asked, "Your Majesty, will you marry me?"

Holey cheese, I couldn't believe my ears! Stella cried, "Yes!"

After a moment's celebration, the queen

turned to me and said, "My handsome captain, I'm afraid you and I are just too different — for example, you prefer **flurk** to **goobers**. So I have decided to marry Nova! I hope you're not too heartbroken."

"Your Majesty, I completely agree with you!" I squeaked, trying not to sound too happy.

WHAT A RELIEF. The idea of having to marry Queen Stella had made my fur stand on end!

The queen smiled and announced, *"Tomorrow I will be wed!"*

Everyone cheered.

After a moment, I hesitantly asked, "Um, Your Majesty? Now that you have your crown back, you won't throw us in the flurk, right?"

I ALWAYS DREAMED OF BEING A WRITER!

Luckily, we were not thrown in the flurk. Queen Stella even invited us to her **WEDDING**! And we all got to participate — even Grandfather William and Sally, who came to find us with the **Teletransportix**.

The celebration lasted for three days and three nights.

We danced until we all had **blisters** on our paws!

We sang *alien songs* at the top of our lungs!

We tasted **goobers** prepared in every way imaginable. . . . **Yum!**

We even learned that **SOLAR** and **LUNAR'S** top secret mission had been to find a special fertilizer for the goober plants. So PROFESSOR GREENFUR mixed up a special fertilizer for them right then and there!

The aliens were so happy that they gave us a **FULL LOAD** of flurk. It was a fabumouse trade, since the MouseStar 1 was all out of cheese!

When we finally returned to the *MouseStar 1*, I breathed a sigh of relief. As soon as I opened the door to my cabin I exclaimed, "Solar smoked gouda, I'm finally home!"

I had to smile when I saw the notes for my book waiting on my desk.

I'm not cut out for such danger — I really dream of being a writer.

Right then, I decided that I would add a new chapter to my book, based on our trip to planet Flurkon. I hope you enjoyed reading it!

Until next time, my dear mouse friends. You can bet your whiskers I'm looking forward to my next stellar adventure!

See you next time!

Be sure to read all my fabumouse adventures!

#1 Lost Treasure of the Emerald Eye

#2 The Curse of the Cheese Pyramid

#3 Cat and Mouse in a Haunted House

#4 I'm Too Fond of My Fur!

#5 Four Mice Deep in the Jungle

#6 Paws Off, Cheddarface!

#7 Red Pizzas for a Blue Count

#8 Attack of the Bandit Cats

#9 A Fabumouse Vacation for Geronimo

#10 All Because of a Cup of Coffee

#11 It's Halloween, You 'Fraidy Mouse!

#12 Merry Christmas, Geronimo!

#13 The Phantom of the Subway

#14 The Temple of the Ruby of Fire

#15 The Mona Mousa Code

#16 A Cheese-Colored Camper

#17 Watch Your Whiskers, Stilton!

#18 Shipwreck on the Pirate Islands

#19 My Name Is Stilton, Geronimo Stilton

#20 Surf's Up, Geronimo!

#21 The Wild, Wild West

#22 The Secret of Cacklefur Castle

A Christmas Tale

#23 Valentine's Day Disaster

#24 Field Trip to Niagara Falls

#25 The Search for Sunken Treasure

#26 The Mummy with No Name

#27 The Christmas Toy Factory

#28 Wedding Crasher

#29 Down and Out Down Under

#30 The Mouse Island Marathon

#31 The Mysterious Cheese Thief

Christmas Catastrophe

#32 Valley of the Giant Skeletons

#33 Geronimo and the Gold Medal Mystery

#34 Geronimo Stilton, Secret Agent

#35 A Very Merry Christmas

#36 Geronimo's Valentine

#37 The Race Across America

#38 A Fabumouse School Adventure

#39 Singing Sensation

#40 The Karate Mouse

#41 Mighty Mount Kilimanjaro

#42 The Peculiar Pumpkin Thief

#43 I'm Not a Supermouse!

#44 The Giant Diamond Robbery

#45 Save the White Whale!

#46 The Haunted Castle

#47 Run for the Hills, Geronimo!

#48 The Mystery in Venice

#49 The Way of the Samurai

#50 This Hotel Is Haunted!

#51 The Enormouse Pearl Heist

#52 Mouse in Space!

#53 Rumble in the Jungle

#54 Get into Gear, Stilton!

#55 The Golden Statue Plot

#56 Flight of the Red Bandit

The Hunt for the Golden Book

#57 The Stinky Cheese Vacation

#58 The Super Chef Contest

Don't miss my journey through time!

Meet
GERONIMO STILTONOOT

He is a cavemouse — Geronimo Stilton's ancient ancestor! He runs the stone newspaper in the prehistoric village of Old Mouse City. From dealing with dinosaurs to dodging meteorites, his life in the Stone Age is full of adventure!

#1 The Stone of Fire

#2 Watch Your Tail!

#3 Help, I'm in Hot Lava!

#4 The Fast and the Frozen

#5 The Great Mouse Race

#6 Don't Wake the Dinosaur!

Don't miss these exciting Thea Sisters adventures!

Thea Stilton and the Dragon's Code

Thea Stilton and the Mountain of Fire

Thea Stilton and the Ghost of the Shipwreck

Thea Stilton and the Secret City

Thea Stilton and the Mystery in Paris

Thea Stilton and the Cherry Blossom Adventure

Thea Stilton and the Star Castaways

Thea Stilton: Big Trouble in the Big Apple

Thea Stilton and the Ice Treasure

Thea Stilton and the Secret of the Old Castle

Thea Stilton and the Blue Scarab Hunt

Thea Stilton and the Prince's Emerald

Thea Stilton and the Mystery on the Orient Express

Thea Stilton and the Dancing Shadows

Thea Stilton and the Legend of the Fire Flowers

Thea Stilton and the Spanish Dance Mission

Thea Stilton and the Journey to the Lion's Den

Thea Stilton and the Great Tulip Heist

Thea Stilton and the Chocolate Sabotage

Thea Stilton and the Missing Myth

Be sure to read all of our magical special edition adventures!

THE KINGDOM OF FANTASY

THE QUEST FOR PARADISE:
THE RETURN TO THE KINGDOM OF FANTASY

THE AMAZING VOYAGE:
THE THIRD ADVENTURE IN THE KINGDOM OF FANTASY

THE DRAGON PROPHECY:
THE FOURTH ADVENTURE IN THE KINGDOM OF FANTASY

THE VOLCANO OF FIRE:
THE FIFTH ADVENTURE IN THE KINGDOM OF FANTASY

THE SEARCH FOR TREASURE:
THE SIXTH ADVENTURE IN THE KINGDOM OF FANTASY

THEA STILTON: THE JOURNEY TO ATLANTIS

THEA STILTON: THE SECRET OF THE FAIRIES

THEA STILTON: THE SECRET OF THE SNOW

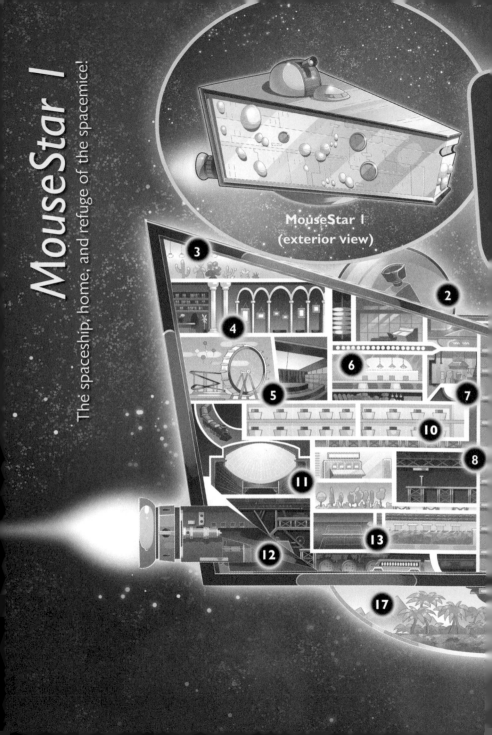

MouseStar 1

The spaceship, home, and refuge of the spacemice!

MouseStar 1
(exterior view)

Dear mouse friends,
thanks for reading,
and good-bye until the next book.
See you in outer space!